My First
MOG ABC

First published in paperback in Great Britain in 2017 by HarperCollins Children's Books.

1 3 5 7 9 10 8 6 4 2

ISBN: 978-0-00-824550-4

HarperCollins Children's Books is a division of HarperCollins Publishers Ltd.

A CIP catalogue record for this book is available from the British Library.

www.harpercollins.co.uk

Printed and bound in China

Aa is for Animals

Bb is for Baby

“Mog loves babies,”
said Mrs Thomas.

Cc is for Cats

Dd is for Dog

Ee is for Egg

Mog enjoys eating eggs.

Ff is for Family

Mog likes
playing in
the garden.

Gg is for Garden

Hh is for Hat

"I think you look
nicer without a hat,"
said Debbie.

Emily doesn't want
an ice-cream.

Ii is for Ice-cream

"Quick
Mog! Jump!"
said the
granny,
and Mog
jumped.

Jj is for Jump

Kk is for Kittens

Mog is licking Tibbles.

Ll is for Lick

Mm is for Mog

Nn is for Night

Oo is for Ow!

"Oh dear!" said Debbie.

Pp is for Playing

Qq is for Queen

All the animals have queued
behind the Queen.

Rr is for Roof

At supper
time Mog
was still
on the roof.

The little fox wants to play
with Mog in the snow!

Ss is for Snow

Tt is for Table

Mog should not be on the table.

Nicky picked
Mog up.

Uu is for Up

The vet tried to
look at Mog, but it
was very difficult.

Vv is for Vet

Mog had to have a wash.

Ww is for Wash

Xx is for Ox

Mog examines an ox.

Yy is for Yuck!

Mog met some
zebras at the zoo.

Zz is for Zoo

Aa Bb Cc Dd Ee
Ff Gg Hh Ii Jj Kk Ll
Mm Nn Oo Pp Qq Rr
Ss Tt Uu Vv Ww Xx
Yy Zz